GW00857291

Text copyright © 1995 Christine Pullein-Thompson
Illustrations copyright © 1995 Peter Clover

First published in 1995

First published in Great Britain in 1995
by Macdonald Young Books
Campus 400
Maylands Avenue
Hemel Hempstead
Herts HP2 7EZ

All rights reserved.

This book is sold subject to the condition that it shall not, by way
of trade or otherwise, be lent, re-sold, hired out, or otherwise
circulated without the publisher's prior consent in any form of
binding or cover other than that in which it is published and
without a similar condition including this condition being imposed
on the subsequent purchaser.

The right of Christine Pullein-Thompson to be identified as the author of
this Work and the right of Peter Clover to be identified as the illustrator
of this Work has been asserted by them in accordance with the
Copyright, Designs and Patents Act 1988.

Typeset in 16/24pt Garamond by Goodfellow & Egan Ltd, Cambridge
Printed and bound in Portugal by Ediçoes ASA

British Library Cataloguing in Publication Data available.

ISBN: 0 7500 1604 3
ISBN: 0 7500 1605 1 (pb)

The Best Pony For Me !

Christine Pullein-Thompson

Illustrated by Peter Clover

MACDONALD YOUNG BOOKS

Chapter One

"I want to ride Honey Bee at the Horse Show and I want to win first prize," said Sophy.

"You will have to ask Mrs Mills about that," Mum said. Mrs Mills ran the riding school where Sophy rode every Saturday.

Sophy made a face. "And I'll need a dark blue coat with a scarlet lining, Mum," she continued, eating a crumpet.

Next day they went to the riding school. Mrs Mills was busy, but straight away Sophy said, "I want Honey Bee for the Horse Show. All right?"

"I want, I want, I want," replied Mrs Mills. "Why don't you say 'please can I have' for a change, Sophy?"

"Sorry, but please can I have Honey Bee for the Horse Show?" asked Sophy.

"The answer is no, Sophy, because you're having Mousie," replied Mrs Mills firmly.

"Not Mousie! Oh no, I want a better pony than that," groaned Sophy. "Who's having Honey Bee, then?"

"Claire," replied Mrs Mills, disappearing into a loose box.

"But she's no better than me. It isn't fair," cried Sophy.

Claire and Sophy were enemies. They fought over stable forks and dandy brushes. Claire thought that she knew everything there was to know about horses. She rode Saturdays *and* Sundays. Sophy thought that Claire was Mrs Mills' favourite pupil.

She was really upset now. She followed Mrs Mills into the loose box, which had a large grey horse inside, and asked, "If Claire gets a cold, can I ride Honey Bee, please?"

But before Mrs Mills could reply Claire appeared, and, giving Sophy a little push, said, "I shall ride her whatever happens, stupid."

"Supposing you have measles?" asked Sophy.
"I shall still ride," said Claire.

"But everyone else will catch it then," replied Sophy, making a face at Claire.

"Not if I'm in the open air," said Claire, making a rude face back.

"What if you break your arm?" asked Sophy next.

"I shall ride with it in a sling," said Claire.
"And drop all the potatoes in the potato race!"
"No I won't, I'll carry them in my sling,
tupid. Anyway, I don't care if I do drop them.
 don't care about *anything* as long as I have
Honey Bee for the Show," replied Claire.
    And Sophy had no answer to that!

Sophy spent the next hour practising for the Show. First she rode Mousie round and round in a pretend Family Pony Class. Mousie was what Mrs Mills called 'slow but sure'. And when they practised the potato race Claire and Honey Bee won easily. Claire held her arms up in triumph, while Sophy dismounted to pick up the potatoes she had dropped.

Mrs Mills said, "Well done, Claire. Bad luck, Sophy. You need to improve your aim."

When Mum collected Sophy from the riding
school she said, "Good news! I've got you a
navy coat with a scarlet lining."

Sophy hugged Mum before she said, "I don't
think I'm going to win anything. Mousie's such
a slow old thing, and I dropped half my
potatoes. Mrs Mills said I need to improve
my aim."

15

Mum said, "Why don't you practise at home then, love?" So that evening Sophy put the kitchen bucket on the stairs and tried throwing potatoes over the banisters into it. At first she kept missing, but gradually she improved. Mum wanted the potatoes for supper, but Sophy said,

"I can't stop now. I'm getting better and better. I really am, Mum. Please let me go on."

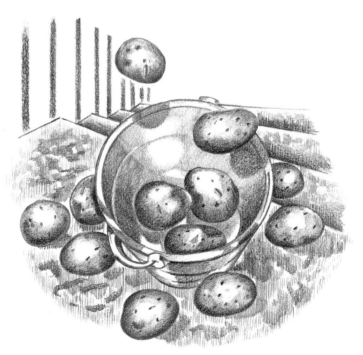

So, though Dad grumbled, they ate rice instead

When Sophy was in bed, Mum and Dad sat wondering what they could do to help her.

"It's really sad, because she wants to win a prize so much," Mum said.

"On the slowest pony at the school – that's really tough," replied Dad, who also liked winning. "Shall I speak to Mrs Mills about it?"

Mum shook her head and said, "That will only make things worse. Mrs Mills is as obstinate as a mule, and well, to be honest, she doesn't get on with Sophy."

"So we really can't do anything to help the poor kid," sighed Dad.

Chapter Two

Next day Sophy groomed Mousie ready for the Show. He was a mousie colour except for his legs, mane and tail which were black. His tail was very thick and full of corkscrews, which took ages to untangle, and his mane had burrs in it which were hard to get out. Claire showed no signs of being ill and she and Sophy only said things like, "Pass me this", or "Pass me that", to one another.

Honey Bee was soon a gleaming gold with her two fetlocks as white as snow. Claire said that tomorrow, unlike Mousie, her pony's mane would be plaited, and Honey Bee would be wearing a new blue headcollar with her name on it.

Sophy stayed silent until Mrs Mills said, 'You're very quiet today, Sophy. Are you sure you are all right? We don't want you ill tomorrow."

"With measles," laughed Claire.

Ignoring Claire, Sophy said, "Please can you tell me, Mrs Mills, why Mousie will be wearing such a crabby old headcollar tomorrow and Honey Bee a lovely new one?"

"Because Mousie isn't a show pony," replied Mrs Mills.

"What is he, then?" asked Sophy.

"Just a reliable old plodder," replied Mrs Mill

And Sophy, who was growing fond of Mousi thought, "So she has favourites among the poni too! No wonder Claire was given Honey Bee!"

"So now you know. Are you still expecting to win a prize?" sneered Claire.

Sophy felt tears rising in her eyes, because suddenly everything seemed so unfair, but she swallowed them and said rather grandly, "Not any more, because I don't think Mousie cares about winning and I don't care much either."

"Liar," said Claire. "You know you do. You know you really *do* want to win a bright red rosette."

When Sophy was at home again she tried on her riding clothes to make sure that they were still all right. She found a speck of dirt on her riding hat, and rubbed it off with a scouring pad. She polished her boots with a duster. She hardly ate anything at teatime.

Looking worried, Mum said, "If you carry on like this, Sophy, you'll never go to another Show."

Dad put his arms around Sophy and said, "You go out there and win. You know you can. You show them," which made Sophy feel worse than ever.

At last the morning of the Show arrived.
Sophy lay in bed, worrying. She worried so
much that she got a headache and couldn't eat
any breakfast. For however hard she tried not
to worry, deep down inside, Sophy still wanted
to win first prize.

Looking at her drawn face, Mum wished that Sophy wasn't going to the Show. She wished that she had never taken up riding. She wished she would stay at home and ride her bike round and round the Close, and play with her cat, Tabby, and her poor neglected dolls.

When Sophy was dressed for the Show Dad said that she looked like a proper little rider. He said that he was proud of her already, and if she won a rosette he would put a fiver in her money box.

When they reached the showground it was crowded with people. Mousie was tied to a fence. He was still wearing his crabby old headcollar and was tacked up ready for her. Sophy felt really weak now. Her legs were like jelly and there were butterflies in her stomach.

Mum hugged her. She looked at her glum face and said, "Oh, darling, it's meant to be fun," before Mrs Mills called, "Hurry up, dear. I'm waiting for you."

Dad tied a large number to Sophy's left arm. It was Number 77. He pulled up Mousie's girth and helped her mount. "Best of luck," he said.

Looking proud, Claire led the way into the ing on Honey Bee. She was wearing a tweed acket which looked just right for the occasion.

After trotting round and round the ring for ten minutes or more Sophy and a boy called Ollie were called into the middle by a Steward with a microphone. Sophy's spirits soared.

"We're first and second, aren't we?" she cried hopefully. "We've won."

Ollie laughed and laughed. "We haven't won," he said. "We're in the back row, and we'll be sent out soon. We're the 'no goods', silly. Poor old Pieman never wins but I don't care."

Ollie leaned forward to pat the piebald pony he was riding. "I still love him. I don't want any other pony, not ever. To me he'll always be the greatest. And I like the pony you're riding. He looks the sort who would never let you down."

"But he won't win anything," replied Sophy glumly as other riders joined them.

"Who cares about winning? It's only a show, for goodness sake. I just come for the fun," Ollie said.

But Sophy still wished that she was with the riders lining up in the front row, and now she was sure she wouldn't be, not ever.

Soon she, Ollie and the rest of the riders in the back row were sent out of the ring. Sophy joined Mum and Dad. "I do love Mousie, but it seems he isn't the right shape to win prizes," Sophy said.

Dad looked disappointed. "I'm going to speak to Mrs Mills. Next time you're going to ride Honey Bee or we go elsewhere," he said.

While the judging continued, Sophy rode right around the showground on Mousie. And suddenly she loved seeing his mealy brown neck and his pricked ears in front of her. She loved looking over people's heads. And the creak of the saddle. Suddenly just to be riding Mousie seemed enough. She didn't need to win prizes as well.

Later Mrs Mills said, "Bad luck, Sophy. I think Mousie is a perfect family pony, but it seems the judge didn't agree with me."

"It's all right, I don't mind," replied Sophy, surprised. Then she put her arms around Mousie's neck and told him that like Pieman, he was the greatest pony in the world. Mousie looked surprised, because no one had ever told him that before!

Chapter Three

Sophy was put among the little ones for her
first heat in the potato race.

"You go for it," said Dad, helping her to line
up. There were dads and mums and elder sisters
ready to run with nearly all the other riders.

Mum called, "Good luck," then they were off.

Mousie would only trot from potato holder to bucket and back again. Luckily it was a very fast trot, faster than the mums and dads and elder sisters could run. After so much practice Sophy's potatoes fell straight into the bucket.

"Well done, Number 77. You've won. Wait in the corner over there," called the judge.

"Bravo," called Dad, ducking under the ring ropes to pat Mousie.

Claire was in the corner already. She said, "I've won my heat too, so we'll be together in the final. And you won't have a chance, because your heat was easy-peasy to win. The final will be much harder, especially with me in it. So don't be upset if you're last, will you, Sophy? Don't cry."

Patting Mousie, Sophy said, "I don't care about winning, not even a teeny weeny bit."

"Liar," said Claire.

"Are you ready. Get ready. Get set. *Go!*" cried the starter. Honey Bee was away first, as fast as a streak of lightning. Sophy kicked Mousie with her heels, but he would only trot.

Up and down he went like clockwork, slow clockwork. Sophy could hear Dad calling, "Wake him up, Sophy. Get him going. Kick him along."

Once again Sophy did not miss the bucket, but she was still collecting her last potato as Claire held up her arms in triumph crying, "I'm first. I've won!"

Sophy almost gave up then, but the judge called, "Keep going. Don't stop, dear. Drop your last potato in. Good girl."

"It's over," thought Sophy as she rode out of the ring. "The Show is over for me and Claire has won again."

"Well done, you were slow but sure," said Mum as Sophy dismounted.

"If only old Mousie would put his skates on," complained Dad. "He really *is* a plodder."

Claire was waiting to go into the ring to receive another red rosette. Her eyes were shining with triumph. Then an amazing thing happened. Approaching Sophy, the judge said, "You're first, Number 77. Well done!"

"But I can't be. It must be a mistake. I was way behind the others," replied Sophy. "Didn't you see – I was last."

Patting Mousie, the judge said in a loud voice, "The little girl on Honey Bee missed the bucket with her last potato. When we looked there were only three potatoes in her bucket instead of four. And the other three competitors missed too, though they put them in eventually. So you're first, Number 77. Hurry up, we haven't got all day."

Claire started to shout then. "It isn't fair. Why didn't someone tell me I had missed? If they had I would have got off and put the last potato in the bucket and still won because I was miles ahead of everyone else. Someone *complain*. Where's the manager? It isn't fair."

But no one listened to her, not even Mrs Mills who seemed delighted by Sophy's win.

So Sophy rode in first on plain little Mousie.

"You have a very good aim, dear," said the judge, handing Sophy a red rosette and a small brown envelope. "Did you practise a lot?"

"Yes, on the stairs at home," replied Sophy.

"Well, it paid off," laughed the judge, patting Mousie.

Claire was beating the ground with her riding whip in a terrible rage as Sophy rode Mousie round the ring on a lap of honour. And this time he cantered all the way.

As she rode out, Ollie put his thumbs up and called, "Well done!"

Then Dad attached the red rosette to Mousie's bridle while Sophy opened the small brown envelope. Inside was five pounds. "But I didn't expect a prize as well as a rosette," Sophy said.

"What will you do with the money?" asked Mum, patting Mousie.

And straight away Sophy knew. "I'll buy Mousie a beautiful blue headcollar with his name on it," she said.

"And if there's any money left, lots and lots of carrots for him. Unless you want me to pay some money towards the blue coat, Mum?" she added.

Mum laughed and said, "It's going back tonight. I only borrowed it."

Then, looking at Dad, Sophy said, "If you're really giving me five pounds, Dad, please don't put it in my money box, put it towards an extra riding lesson for me. And please don't ask Mrs Mills about Honey Bee. Mousie's the best pony for me now. All right?"

"All right. And well done!" Dad said.

Sophy knew now that it had been the best day of her life, not just because she had won, but also because she had enjoyed riding more than ever before. But most of all because Mousie would now have his very own blue headcollar with his name on it and then he would feel every bit as good as Honey Bee.

Look out for other books in the Storybooks series:

I Want That Pony! by Christine Pullein-Thompson

Sophy loves Flash, the pony that lives down the lane. But the pony belongs to somebody else, who doesn't want to let Sophy have anything to do with her beloved pony . . .

Alice Alone by Shirley Isherwood

Alice and her little brother Scooter love staying on their grandfather's farm. But one night Grandfather is very late coming home – is anything wrong?

A Magic Birthday by Adèle Geras

Maddy can't wait until her birthday party. All her special friends are coming and there is going to be a conjuring show. But Maddy is worried that there will be one important thing missing . . .

The Laughing Snowman by Anne Forsyth

During the snow, Emma is woken up in the middle of the night by the sound of laughter. And when she peeks outside, she sees the most astonishing sight!

Khumalo's Blanket by Iain Macdonald

Khumalo's village is in danger, and he must choose between his most treasured possession and the good of all his people.

Storybooks can be ordered from your local bookshop, or they can be ordered straight from the publisher. For more information, write to: *The Sales Department, M Young Books, Campus 400, Maylands Avenue, Hemel Hempstead HP2 7EZ.*